Praise for *Chicago Stories*

"Mike Czyzniejewski's *Chicago Stories* reads at once as scatting celebration of the moral landscape that stretches across the country's midsection, and as a travelogue. Czyzniejewski's sharp wit and peering eye trek along that crooked road between the dead president & crony highways and the murky river, crossing tracks where trains haven't run in two score—before boring down past the juke joints sidled against public houses, and corner hustlers hawking whores to blue pickpockets and last migrants on the run, down where they all keep score in shadow votes. The author brings it home early and often here as, along with so much more, he is a sojourner."

—Bayo Ojikutu, author of *Free Burning*

"In *Chicago Stories,* Michael Czyzniejewski channels Studs Terkel's Division Street, the voices so singular and complete that in the end you feel as though you've listened to each story rather than read them. Rob Funderburk's illustrations are a snapshot of movement; in their messy, deliberate lines each voice comes alive. Chicago buffs: if you like architecture, that is, if you like outsides, the riverboat tour will do. But if you're looking to go inside for a deeper look, Czyzniejewski's book will take you there."

—Lindsay Hunter, author of *Daddy's*

"In the surreal, comic world of Michael Czyzniejewski's *Chicago Stories,* where Twitter leads to crack babies and Dennis Rodman has directly influenced every sorority girl's drunkenly obtained tattoo, somehow the very real Chicago—with its highways, skyline, stadiums and scandalous celebrities—lovingly infuses every line."

—Gina Frangello, author of *Slut Lullabies* and *My Sister's Continent*

"Carl Sandburg wrote of Chicago, 'Come and show me another city with lifted head singing so proud to be alive and coarse and strong and cunning.' Michael Czyzniejewski offers up his own glorious, fabulist interpretation of this alive and coarse and strong and cunning city on the make in his wonderful *Chicago Stories.* Czyzniejewski is a pointillist, serving up one intriguing, isolated moment in Chicago's history after another, but when you finish this book and take a step back, you see the whole bustling city for what it is: absurd, heartbreaking, tough, and vibrant. It's really quite an accomplishment."

—John McNally, author of *After the Workshop* and *Ghosts of Chicago*

"In *Chicago Stories,* Michael Czyzniejewski summons all of Chicago—its ghosts, living and dead, its heroes and fools, sinners and saints, its people and places and all of its occasions—and in these pages they have gathered, strange and unlikely bedfellows, to sing a new song for Chicago. It will twist your arm behind your back, this song. It will break your fingers."

—Billy Lombardo, author of *The Man With Two Arms* and *The Logic of a Rose: Chicago Stories*

"Michael Czyzniejewski encapsulates all of Chicago's past, present and future with his big-shouldered prose, channeling Cubs hall-of-famer Ron Santo, former mayor Jane Byrne, and even the venerable Water Tower herself in voices both wise and funny."

—Allison Amend, author of *Stations West*

"An absurdist Chi-town *Spoon River Anthology* on crack, Mike Czyzniejewski's *Chicago Stories* is an explosion of imagination, a relentless churn of intellect and wit. In true Chicago style, this book tells it straight to your face and pulls no punches."

—Alan Heathcock, author of *VOLT*

Also by Michael Czyzniejewski

Elephants in Our Bedroom: Stories

CHICAGO STORIES

40 Dramatic Fictions

BY MICHAEL CZYZNIEJEWSKI

CURBSIDE SPLENDOR, CHICAGO

CURBSIDE SPLENDOR PUBLISHING

Published by Curbside Splendor Publishing, Inc., Chicago, Illinois, in 2012.

First Edition.

Grateful acknowledgement is made to *Another Chicago Magazine, Artifice, The Collagist, Knee-Jerk, Make, The Nervous Breakdown, Ninth Letter Online, The Packingtown Review,* and *Requited,* where many of these stories first appeared. See page 151 for complete listing. "From the Grave, Carl Sandburg Workshops the Author's Manuscript (sans this last page)" owes a large debt to Carl Sandburg's poem, "Chicago."

The writing of *Chicago Stories* was supported in part by an award from the National Endowment for the Arts.

ART WORKS.
arts.gov

Library of Congress Control Number: 2012931479

ISBN 978-0-9834228-5-3

Designed and illustrated by Rob Funderburk.
Edited by Jacob S. Knabb.
Manufactured in the United States of America.

www.curbsidesplendor.com

Table of Contents

For Dolly

First person I ever met in Chicago.

CHICAGO STORIES

40 Dramatic Fictions

Mrs. O'Leary's Ghost Comforts Steve Bartman at the Ruins of Meigs Field

Sisyphus, we're told, relished the moments when the boulder rolled back down, enough time to wipe his brow, examine the birds, crank his neck in its socket and savor the crack. Atlas took a breather, duped Hercules into assuming the burden, at least until Hercules duped him into taking it back. Pope Sixtus IV approved the Inquisition, but tried to recant when things got out of hand. Truman killed two cities with a nod, but when he ran for reelection, his legacy became an alleged defeat. Myself, I take solace in the Water Tower, how the city had a chance to start over, become a vanguard of architecture, science, and industry. How rats run amok in the Big Apple, but not in our fair streets. How our garbage sits in alleys instead of out on the sidewalks. How that cow never gave much milk, anyway, and the shoes I made from her skin were the most comfortable I'd ever worn. How tender her meat was, bloody and thick, the taste of guilt bleeding from every bite.

Barack Obama Describes His Perfect Bowling Game to the Graduating Class, Arizona State University Commencement, 2029

I hadn't seen that many turkeys in a row since my first White House Thanksgiving dinner. It takes twelve straight strikes to roll a perfect game, but if you would have asked me that the last time I stood on this stage, I wouldn't have known. If you would have asked me that in 2016, I wouldn't have known then, either. Richard Nixon put an alley in the basement and I replaced it with a hoops court. It was a new era. I was trying to make a statement. And at the time, I could still go to the hole. Fast forward eight years, eight long years, and it would seem I had nothing left to accomplish. My resume, even by the harshest of standards, appeared, at long last, flawless. Needless to say, I still had goals. Every man is haunted by something, and my ghost lived in Altoona, Pennsylvania, on a sound stage in Burbank, California. I joined a league. I rolled, at first, one night a week, then two, then three and four, until I was bowling four hours a day, every day. I hired coaches. I had the best equipment. I was obsessed. Then, three months ago, during an elimination bracket, tourney semifinals, everything clicked. I started well, felt good, but wasn't watching the score screen, not until that first bird gobbled down at me from his perch. I'd never started with a turkey, and by the time the second appeared, I knew this was going to be a special game. I never even broke a sweat, not when the first reporter showed up and started filming, not when the ten pin almost wobbled back in place in the eighth frame. The moment I released that twelfth ball—what some might call the defining moment of my post-presidential career—I just knew, knew that it would find the pocket, that the pins would scatter, that I'd be the first black ex-president to accomplish this particular feat. Then, when the screen flashed *300* over and over, when Lou, the alley owner, showed me the place on the wall where my name would be etched in brass, when I called Michelle and she broke into tears, I knew that I had put the ghosts to rest, that I had answered my critics. That I had, at long last, provided a complete body of work.

John Wentworth Defends the Potential Awesomeness of Chicago, Wisconsin

Imagine the city's border stretching all the way from Kankakee on the south end to Green Bay on the north. It would have been an oasis seen from the tiptop of the Rocky Mountains, its light drowning out Detroit, St. Louis, even New York City, its clamorous commerce and commotion audible from London, from Paris, all the way from China. Just picture the map, the large, fierce blob hugging the west coast of Lake Michigan, a baby clinging to its mother's teat. Hear the roars of the crowds, stadia toiling with hundreds of thousands, Banks and Aaron hitting three-four, Oscar dishing to Michael, Favre handing off to Walter. Taste the encased meats, feel their juices bursting in your mouth, Hog Butcher of World supplying Sausagetown, USA. Combine the Taste with Summerfest, our ingenuity with their hominess. It could have been the greatest city in the world. Nothing against the fine folks to the south: the Peorians, the Normals, the Metropolins, but all that dairy! The Dells! Skiing! And the cheese, the fucking cheese! We still did a pretty good job, neither city anything to be ashamed of, but something special was in our grasp. We could have called it Chicaukee, better than Milcago (or Milwaugo), if you had to pick one, though believe me, I was shoveling and wrecking to keep the whole thing Chicago—because I would have been senator,

I could have made things like that happen. It's probably too late now, me dead, the Chicago machine firmly in place, state borders set and secure. But it's worth remembering, worth dreaming about. Worth more than a crooked street along a highway.

Ann Landers Advises Against the Use of Twitter

This isn't like the razorblades in the apples. Or the rice making pigeons explode. Or my sister's alleged "talent." This, faithful readers, is real. While it seems like 140 characters could do no actual harm, studies—by Harvard doctors and scientists—have proven that prolonged use of and exposure to the Internet website known as "Twitter" is today's primary cause of teenage pregnancy. Of course, our children are not having babies simply because they log on ... though with all that can be found on this World Wide Web, you could see how it could happen. It's the life path that Tweeting—so it is known—can lead them down. One Tweet leads to another, and before you know it, our children are listening more closely to their followers than their parents. What's next? What's after teenage pregnancy? The inevitable: crack babies. Yes, logging onto Twitter, according to those same Harvard doctors and scientists, has led to young pregnant girls—the very pregnant girls who became pregnant on Twitter—smoking crack and passing addiction down to their unborn fetuses. I don't know if you have ever seen a crack baby, let alone a neglected crack baby, but it's not an encouraging sight. Just imagine if that was your grandchild. Then what happens when these child-parents want to go back to school? To a football game? To prom? Either you're stuck watching their babies while they're out gallivanting or they start leaving their babies in Dumpsters, in broken-down elevators, and, sometimes, fire stations. Is that what we want? Parents, it's time you took control back, said no to your children once in a while, spent quality time nurturing them, showing them the right way. They need human-on-human contact, not this cyberspace interaction they've grown accustomed to. And if some teacher or guidance counselor or friend wants to stand in your way? Watch it, bub! The next thing we know, the abandoned crack baby who calls you "Grammy" will replace some poor Dalmatian as the official mascot down at the local firehouse. Mark my word.

Speaking at the Calumet City Chamber of Commerce Annual Luncheon, Gary Dotson Tells Tale of Inspiration and Longing

A three-legged dog was hitchhiking on the southbound Dan Ryan this morning, and since I know a thing or two about bad breaks, I stopped and gave the poor fella a ride. He jumped right up on the passenger seat, never once letting on he had a handicap, other than needing me to open and shut the door for him (his front right leg was the one missing, in case you're wondering). My only request was, "If you gotta go, let me know, and I'll pull over." The three-legged dog said nothing, and we were on our way. Right about at the split off to the Skyway, I asked my new friend if I could practice my speech, told him how I was invited to come down and talk to you all here today. Since he offered no objections, I ripped into her. That speech, one I knew well enough to recite in my sleep, told another story, that of a man, true in his heart, true to his friends and family, to God and country. I think most of you know what happened to this man, despite his chaste heart, all the trials he endured, the hardships, and his hard-fought vindication. It's an old story, one I'm sure you're familiar with, and I don't think I'll repeat it to you here today. But none of you, I'm guessing, know the story of this three-legged hitchhiking dog. So anyway, after I get done practicing my speech, I asked this dog if he was at all inspired by my words, if he thought my story would make an impression on you fine businessmen who have so graciously invited me to your fabulous soiree. Nothing. My new friend once again sat still, not saying a word, staring out the open window, the breeze blowing through his muzzle like the Holy Spirit Himself was passing through his head. Getting the message pretty quick, I drove on in silence, not even listening to the radio, all the way to the exit to your fine city, assuming my new friend was not impressed. I got to wondering if perhaps I should telephone you nice people and cancel. After all, if I can't impress a three-legged hitchhiking dog, then how were you folks gonna react? However, there is a happy ending. When we reached stoplight at the end of the highway interchange, the three-legged hitchhiking dog turned to me, licked me on the cheek, then leapt out the open window, taking off like a bitch in heat. I called after him, again convinced I'd done something to offend him, but soon saw what he was after: a stray cat out on the sidewalk, strutting her stuff like she owned the place. I won't describe here what the dog did to that cat when he caught up to it, but I think you get the picture. In any case, what I'd like to express to you folks today is a simple lesson, one I hope you'll all take to heart. And that lesson is, when you've lost the means to unlock the door, find the open window and dive on through.

Jean Baptiste Point du Sable Settles at the Mouth of the Cuyahoga River

Imagine a skyline with buildings so tall, you could see them from Buffalo. Imagine the captains of industry centered in the downtown, USG and McDonald's and Kraft, Motorola and Boeing and United. Think halls of fame—of blues and jazz and gospel—forming a mall with rock 'n roll. Picture the parks, lush and expansive, safe and inviting, a bushy green beard for Erie's chin. Envision the Flats, only larger, sporting better restaurants, more famous celebrities, music flowing out of every door. See history, Olympics and World's Fairs and Conventions, assassinations and parades and news reels. Visualize University Circle, the Nobel Prizes, the Manhattan Project, the first Heisman Trophy. Perceive the river green on St. Patty's Day, on fire not at all. Forget "Mistake by the Lake," unless you're talking about someplace else. Imagine the lights, lit all night, never a reason to turn them out. Imagine the sky, a bit clearer and bluer, a bit easier to breathe. Imagine the state quarter, the state symbol, the state slogan. Most of all, imagine Jordan getting that inbounds pass, changing direction, pulling the ball off the dribble and erecting his body into perfect verticality. Chicago Stadium holds its breath as the ball rolls off Michael's fingers, trajecting in a perfect arc, swishing home, Michael jumping in elation, pounding his fist into the air, his jersey white instead of red, his chest emblazoned with an orange CAVS, glowing like a miracle on an already-bright horizon.

Dennis Rodman Envisions His Final Tattoo

People forget I started a revolution. Before me, the NBA was clean, as in Larry Bird clean. John Stockton clean. David Robinson clean. Arms, necks, backs, chests: all blank slates, the kind of players you watched on Christmas, on Mother's Day, the image the Association was selling. College graduates in little boy pants running pick and rolls, making bounce passes, the game below the rim as much as above it. Sure, that league sold tickets, people watched, little suburban boys had posters on their bedroom walls. The Golden Age, you could call it, Dream Teams, kids in the front row, five white guys at the end of every bench. But then I came along, dumped a bottle of peroxide on my head, showed some ink, and all of a sudden, things went to hell. I got three more rings, sure, but those were Jordan's teams—Jordan made everything OK. As soon as he left, they ran me out of town. It was time for a new breed of star, something younger, more pure. But you know what? Every one of those guys had ink, and lots of it, too. Kobe? Ink. Shaq? Ink. And three titles. I was gone, but I'd made my mark, infected everything and everyone. And not just the league. Your sons with the barbed wires on their biceps. Your daughters with the funky designs on their lower backs. All of you with Chinese letters for no damn good reason. Before me, tube socks. After me, sorority girls in the chair, sobbing, drunk, and getting inked, in a neighborhood they don't belong in, out way past their bedtime. I'm in the basketball Hall, but I still don't get enough credit. I changed things. No one thinks twice when they go to the Walmart and the checkout boy is green and blue and black from head to toe, rings in his nose and ears and places you can't see. It's all like getting a haircut now. Everyone's doing it—everyone but me. I haven't had work done in years. There's not room, you might guess, none of me left, but that's not true: Look at that Anderson kid. Now that's going too far. Even I'd tell him to cool it. For me, it would be imitating the imitators. What's the point in that? Yet, before I go—admit it: not many of you thought I'd make it this far—I want one more. I can picture it, my last dance, my coda: a set of bright red lips, as brilliant a red as they can make it. I'll go back every six months to have it touched up, just to keep it as blinding a red as it can be. Where? Square on my ass, right cheek, centered up. It will remind me of what you should all do. Don't worry if you're afraid to get too close—you can blow your kiss my way. Aim well, but if you miss—and everyone misses—don't worry: I'll snatch it clean out of the air and get you another shot.

Tired of the Spaceship Comparisons, the New Soldier Field Responds to Its Critics

Captain Kirk is not the quarterback for the Chicago Bears. Neither is Luke Skywalker, Buck Rogers, or George freakin' Jetson. I do not possess the power to detach myself from the old columned foundation, turn on my thrusters, and disappear in a flash of light. Ambassadors from other planets do not convene on my concourse, and not once, in my short history, has anyone ever phoned me to pick him up and take him home. Furthermore, a funkadelic master has never lured me to Earth with his slinky rhythms, and nothing has ever, on my watch, been stuck up anyone's ass for the advancement of intergalactic knowledge. My coworkers are not small and green, nor are they hell-bent on meeting the drivers of pickup trucks returning to their trailers out in the middle of the desert. I cannot bend the laws of physics, nor can I travel through time. Warp speed is out of the question, especially with a union workforce. All of my materials can be found on our Periodic Table of the Elements, though if you're looking to point fingers, ask the Metrodome what comprises her artificial turf. I do not shy away from black holes. Less than 3 percent of me is painted silver. The term "space-age polymers" is just an expression. On the bright side, no one is buried in my end zone, and I'm not named for a corrupt utilities broker. When it comes right down to it, you'd have to admit, you wouldn't ask about any of this if the boys were making a go of it, the scoreboard singing a happier song. If Butkus or the Coach were still here. Or, God rest his soul, Walter. If Brett Favre were running for his life, the microphones picking up the crack of his bones. His head bouncing off my hard earth, his mind on a brief mission to Mars.

Jane Byrne Discusses Edward Hopper's *Nighthawks* With Her New Neighbors, Cabrini-Green, 1981

My father used to say that he was the man you could only see from behind, the man sitting alone on one end of the counter in the gray suit. He told me he never knew anyone was capturing him, finishing his coffee and reading the late edition, waiting to make his move. It must have been 10 or 11 at night, he said, because that's the time Phillies became his haunt. My father was never home at night, and when he was, could never sleep, so it all made sense to me. I was young. I believed him. The next part was harder to swallow, but it was my favorite part, so I never let on I doubted him in any way. After my father told me he was the man you could only see from behind, waiting to make his move, he explained that the redhead in the red dress, sitting next to the guy in the blue suit, was my mother, that the night Hopper was inspired by this scene was the night they met and fell in love. Right after Hopper took the visual snapshot of my father from across the street, the artist must have left, because moments later, my father would rise, walk around the counter, and ask my mother if she'd marry him. Right there, never meeting her before, right in front of this other guy. "I wish Hopper would've stuck around to see that young man deck me," my father said, not to mention when my mother accepted the proposal, kissed him on the mouth for a minute. But Dad was happy enough to be immortalized just prior to the most crucial moment of his life, if not at the exact moment. Years later, when I realized the timing was off, that Hopper painted *Nighthawks* in 1942, me already 8, my parents well beyond romantic destiny, I never brought it up to him, even when I found out "Phillies" was a cigar ad, not the name of the restaurant, even when he told the story again and again. I was older, but he was still my father, and I still believed him, every word he said. No matter what color the suit, no matter what color my mother's hair.

During a Brief Commerical Break, Wizzo the Wizard Pitches a Rock Opera/Concept Album to Special Guest Billy Corgan

Instead of a deadly cobra, it's the long, alluring neck of a guitar rising from the basket. That's the opening number, and the album cover, too. Think about it. A young boy living in the streets, no parents, no home, stealing food, sleeping in doorways, picking pockets in and around the public market. His only friend is his cunning, his cunning and the ancient snake charmer who woos serpents outside the carpet dealer's carpet shop. The young boy—played by the lead singer and guitarist, you—sits with the old man several hours a night. He catches snakes in the desert, listens to parables, even shares half the food he steals. In exchange, the snake chamer gives him the only gift he can give, the ability to charm snakes. Somehow, and I haven't figured this out yet, the snakes turn into a guitar, and the young boy learns to play that guitar better than anyone in the world. By the final act, he frees his fellow boy-thieves from some kind of prison, avenges the death of his snake-charming mentor (which happens at the end of Act II), and deposes the tyrannical sheik, earning the hand of his lovely and not-at-all tyrannical young daughter. All by playing this charmed guitar. *Doo-dee doo-dee doo-dee doo-dee do.*

In His Best-Selling Autobiography, Dennis DeYoung Reveals the Origins of "Come Sail Away"

I thought that they were angels—really I did. Right up to the point where they starting shoving that thing up my ass. And we're not talking some delicate instrument, smooth and thin and slathered with K-Y, maybe a little camera on the end. It was more like a mace, a goddamned mace, a thick cube at the end of a crooked stick, metal spikes jutting in every direction. When I first got to the ship, they did some initial testing—temperature, height, weight, etc.—and when they started the probing, they jotted some data down on a legal pad each and every time. There was a set schedule. I was beginning to understand: I had a role, and just hoped they'd take me back to Earth when they were done. But after the first day, something changed. They just did it whenever. The schedule was gone. So was their gentle touch. They used other instruments, things just lying around: a set of ship keys; a lamp; some kind of weird pet with five legs and purple fur on its eyes. They took some pictures, them posing next to my filled backside, like I was Mt. Rushmore and they were on vacation. They seemed to be gambling, too, little blue triangular chips passing back and forth. I smelled booze. By the time they returned me to my studio, I didn't know if I was coming or going. When I tried to work, to block out the experience, something was different. Notes took on tastes, smells. The piano keys were like cinder blocks, all the colors of the rainbow. The air around me felt like waves of an infinite ocean, thick, like a film. My voice floated in the air, flapped in the breeze, took me places outside my body. Like a giant white sail jamming to my groove.

David Yow's 10 Simple Rules for Keeping a Smile on Your Face

1. Become obsessed with serial killers. Read up on as many as you can until you find one to identify with. Become particularly knowledgeable on that person—an expert. In unrelated conversations with friends or family, make comparisons between what they're discussing and your serial killer. If you do this enough times, their reactions will be priceless.

2. Go shirtless as much as possible. Outside of fast-food restaurants and libraries, no laws demand that you wear a shirt, and even those would be hard to defend in court.

3. Be completely honest with everyone you encounter, even if what you say ruins their lives. People will hate you, but they will also stop bothering you with things you don't care about. Refer to yourself as a "straight shooter."

4. Find a hobby, something you like doing, something you're good at, something you'd make into a career if you lost your job, if your family were killed in a car accident, or if you were the victim of a massive head injury. Learn to play bass. Query on space for an art gallery. Cook. If anything should befall you—fired, instant orphan, brain damage—you'll be prepared for your new life, ready to hit the ground running.

5. Have sex with someone or something outside your sexuality, just once, so you can say

that you never limited yourself. Have the sex be unprotected, unless you're a coward. Make up for this by falling in love.

6. Never change your hairstyle or your shoes, just everything in between. People will still recognize you, think of you as a steady, reliable presence, trust you with information you can use against them later (see #3).

7. Call your mother, if she's alive, every day, and your father at least every other day. If they're dead, never waste time visiting their graves. The phone calls were more than enough.

8. Use foul language, especially if you can appall an audience with it. This will focus their hatred of you and help hide all your despicable traits that really matter, those that aren't just sounds coming from your mouth.

9. At least once in your life, show your genitals to someone who's not expecting it. You may get arrested or put on a nefarious list, but once in a while, it might make someone happy. If your genitals can do that for a total stranger, then you've really and truly lived.

10. Floss, avoid red meat, and eat green leafy vegetables, but never, ever let on to anyone that you do so. If anyone finds out, you might as well take your own life.

Gil Scott-Heron Leaves a Voice Mail for R. Kelly, February 3, 2002

You will not hang up. You will not erase this message. You will not know who this is until it doesn't matter anymore, and when you do, you will not care. You will not forget what I've said because you will not stop thinking about it long enough to forget. You will not have that luxury. You will not have any luxury. The sun will not appear to shine in the morning and the night will not come fast enough. Your food will taste as filth and your drink will be dry as sand. Your clothes will not fit. Your air will not be fresh. The records you listen to and the books you read will no longer sound the same. Your accuser will not leave you alone. The police will not leave you alone. The press will not leave you alone. Your fans will not leave you alone, and neither will your wife, your mama, your ladyfriends, or your chaffeur. You will not admit that any of this happened, and I will not speculate about how much of it is true. You will not be sorry, anyway. You will not go on as if nothing happened, whether it did or didn't. Everyone will not believe you. You will not make the same mistake twice, be it these accusations or something else, something forgettable—leaving your socks on the bedroom floor, forgetting to put the milk in the refrigerator, forgetting where you came from and who gave you what you have. The artists who came before you will not like this. The artists who came before you will no longer claim you. The day that everyone forgets all this is so far away, you will not want to know what that date is. You will not always be relevant for what you want to be relevant for. You will not live this down. You will not listen to this entire message. You will not believe you can fly, because if you could, by all means, brother, you would.

Rod Blagojevich Negotiates His First Prison Tattoo, Joliet State Penitentiary

I'd rather you kept my neck out of this. No offense, but I've always considered guys with tattoos all over their fucking necks to have some kind of mental problem. The same goes for the fingers and hands; what kind of dumbfuck walks around with shit written all over their hands? To me, that reveals an essential lack of character, not to mention upbringing. Needless to say, I'd really appreciate if the face were left intact. In terms of what you're going to put, a basic symbol could be nice, maybe a clover or a heart, but since we're looking at all black, probably not. An outline of the fucking state of Illinois could work, for irony, or maybe the four stars and two bars of the Chicago city flag. I'd rather not go with someone's face, as I can't imagine those look good in twenty fucking years, not with all the sagging and wrinkling. In terms of writing, gothic lettering is clichéd. That, and any sort of exaggerated script. You can't even read shit like that unless you're right up on top of the fucking person, and we don't foresee that ever happening, do we? "Mom" would be a sentimental choice, classy, while "Patricia" wouldn't make me look so bad, either. What I really want to fucking avoid, above all else, is anything that would pledge my allegiance to a particular group, or anything that would imply ownership of me by any one of you. You have a golden fucking opportunity here that you can't let go to waste—believe me, I understand—but think of when I'm out of here, when my supporters—and there are still lots of them—vote me back into office. It's only a matter of time before the truth comes out and I'm back on top. When that happens, there could be a job for you. No, on second thought, there *will* be a job for you. All you have to do is make the right decision now. Realize who you're dealing with. Think about your future: It's the code I've always lived by, and as far as I'm concerned, it's a pretty good fucking code.

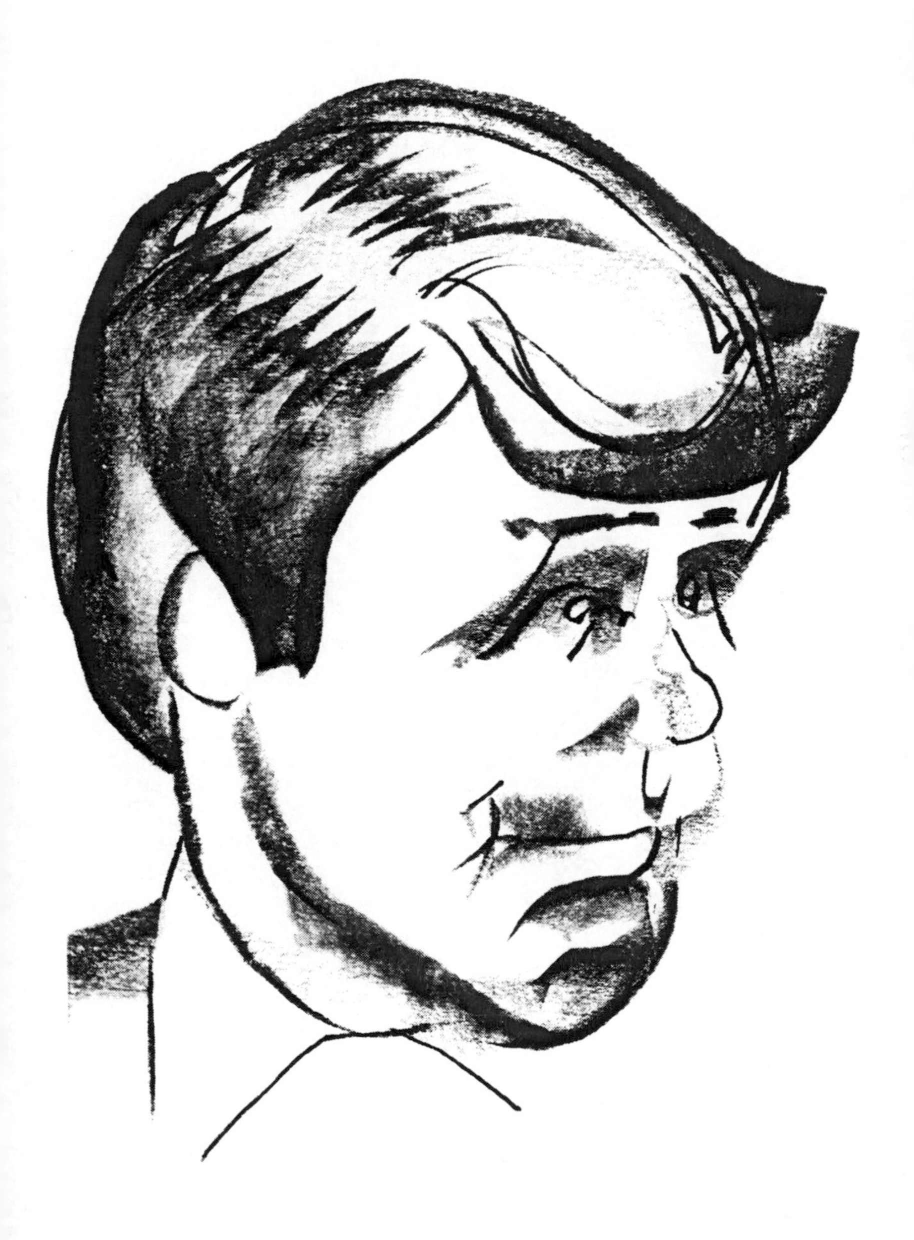

The Ghost of Rosetta Jackson Lobbies Congress to Continue Funding Planned Parenthood

The coat hanger, in my day, did not yet exist. They told me to jump rope, drink this, drink that, and it worked ... on both of us. Today, the coat hanger serves as a symbol for the cause, adorning buttons on lapels and posters during protests. But there's also a lot of talk about this debate not being about abortions, how it concerns education, options, and prevention. Come on. Why can't it be about abortions? Would that be so wrong? All that other stuff is fine, but I don't remember being misinformed. I wasn't disadvantaged. I wasn't ill-prepared. I slept with my sister's husband, over and over again, in their matrimonial bed: Does that sound like I was interested in planning? Would a pamphlet have made any difference? Would a pep talk have kept me chaste and pure? Maybe for other women—I respect that—but I needed things taken care of, a safe place, someone who knew what they were doing. Asking around the neighborhood wasn't the way to go about this, isn't how it should have to be. I wasn't the first teenage girl who made that choice. I wasn't the last. If this goes through, there'll be a lot more. I realized many of you think I got what I deserved, burned from the inside out, nothing less than what was coming to me. It's an interesting stance, one not indefensible. Just remember, most of you will never be in my shoes, will never have to make that decision—and no, it doesn't count if you're the dad, not unless you drink that tea, straighten that hanger, or put your legs in those stirrups and have some hack go to town. I can't believe I've heard men utter the phrase "We're pregnant!" I don't know how they do it with a straight face. What I do know is this: I can't propose a bill. I don't have a vote. It's the way it's always been. The way it still is. Just the way you like it.

Hillary Rodham Clinton Discusses the Hand Over the Mouth

Bill thinks it was allergies. Early May in DC, even down in that room, that's entirely possible. But that wasn't it (though it's sweet of Bill to say so). Allergies are better than what most people say. Most everyone assumes it was shock, a feeble woman at the men's table, watching a bloody gun battle, human life expiring before her eyes. It's as if I were a mother watching her son tackled in a football game. A shopaholic gasping at the price of a mink coat. A romantic discovering a lover's long-withheld secret. It's as if I'd never seen death before or witnessed the brutality of war. It's as if I'd sat there the entire time like that. As if weakness was all I could offer, the males around me bravely taking it in, never shutting their eyes, not shaken by anything, not their first rodeo. If it were a horror movie, one of them—Biden—might have put his arm around me, pulled me close, told me to cover my eyes, swearing he'd tell me when it was over. To put it bluntly, that's bullshit. At that moment, I wasn't aghast. I wasn't in shock. My innocence wasn't slipping away. There was no consternation. Nor was it a yawn, a belch, or any other bodily expulsion. I did not forget to turn off the iron or the oven, the camera snapping as I imagined my house aflame. A breeze had not blown up my skirt. Nobody said anything crude or cruel, offending me. I wasn't eating or taking medication. I wasn't about to throw up. No, the image of me that will outlive me, my defining moment, was none of these. Firstly, there were a lot of pictures taken. In fact, knowing the potential, pictures were constantly being taken. Over the span of ninety minutes, that's a lot of photographs, and of all of them, that photo is the one they decided to release. Didn't one of the men touch his hand to his face at some point? Didn't they all? But none of that matters. What was happening is something that no one has guessed, no one would ever guess. Something was coming out of my mouth, but it wasn't a gasp. It wasn't a cry. What was coming out wasn't something I wanted recorded, not something I wanted the lip-readers to pick up on. They were things I didn't want to be known for, things I didn't want my grandchildren to associate with me. While my male colleagues watched, attentive, silenced, I was having at it. I was the loud one. I was crude. I was the one Barack had to look over at, glancing at me, the cameras, then back at me. I got the picture. After that, when I couldn't hold something in, there was only one way to hide it: the hand over the mouth. I can't be sure of what I was muffling the moment that shot was taken—I said a lot of things that night. But let's assume it was the worst thing I said. Then it was surely the moment that bastard turned and ran, the moment the first bullet took him down. Right before the second one got him in the head, went through his eye and finished him off, I shouted *Shoot that motherfucker in the head,* a flashbulb popping, me lurching forward, my hand keeping everyone guessing, assuming the worst of me, a much different worst than the truth.

Mayor Daley Confronts Frank Gehry in the Men's Room at the Michigan Avenue Bennigan's

It was supposed to look like something I stepped on—only nice. I heard good stuff about you, saw some pictures, permitted you to raise my expectations. I pictured Prague mixed with Bilbao mixed with Düsseldorf, a hint of Seattle thrown in for the young people. My advisors tell me, for all the money I dished out, you didn't even have plans. Just a connect-the-dots doodle on a napkin. Now I'm the last person who's going to tell you how to do your job, but goddamn it, where's the back? It's all front. And don't even get me started on deadlines. I was done with deadlines in 2002. Finished. But now that it's done, I hope you sleep well tonight, knowing what you've done to this project, this city, and most of all, to me. You know, I have a name to live up to here. My old man gave the world JFK. J-F-fucking-K. RFK. Civil Rights. Marilyn on all our birthdays. Let's not forget our very own Picasso, looking down at me every day when I get to work, keeping watch over me as I leave at night. And what have I done? This was supposed to be it, my grand legacy, my gift to the people. *Thank you very much, Junior. At least you tried.* Wipe that smirk off your face and listen to me, mister: What am I supposed to do now? I'll tell you this much: You'll never work in this town again.

In His Berwyn Mayoral Campaign Speech, Rich Koz Sincerely Apologizes to the People of Berwyn

The first thing you need to realize is, nobody's watching. I never said anything derogatory during the Super Bowl, a State of the Union address, or a rerun of *Friends.* I've aired Saturdays, either two in the afternoon or two in the morning, not exactly prime time, and the folks watching TV then aren't the kind of people you need to be image-conscious around. There are literally more of you here now than there are viewers, and that would be true if half of you left to go the bathroom. But enough with the excuses: This is an apology, so the exact number of people who heard you mercilessly mocked, week in and week out, for thirty years, is irrelevant. What's important is that all of it is in good fun. People are laughing with you, not at you. Best of all, most of what I said isn't true—not mostly. Besides: Who outside of Berwyn would even know what a Berwyn was if not for me? Imagine, all these years, that voice moaning, "Elk Grove Village" instead. Or "Schaumburg." Or "Harvey." "Minooka." "Beecher." Berwyn is on the map. Berwyn sings. Berwyn is where it's at. How does any of this make me qualified to be your mayor? It doesn't. But it reminds me of a story:

> Once upon a time, three monsters walk into a bar: a Mummy, a Frankenstein, and a Creature from the Black Lagoon. They sit down and the bartender says, "What can I getcha?" The

Mummy, his face wrapped in bandages, can't speak, so he wails and points at the whiskey, and the bartender pours him a shot. The Frankenstein, he can't speak either, so he grunts and waves his hand toward the beer taps, and the bartender pours him a cold one. Finally, the Creature from the Black Lagoon, he could never speak, so the bartender pours him a glass of white wine and says, "So, Miss, what part of Berwyn did you grow up in?"

BERWYN!

Thank you, folks! And don't forget: Vote Koz!

The Sixteen-Inch Softball Buys a Shot of Malort for the Italian Beef Sandwich at the End of the Bar

Don't take this the wrong way: I got a wife and kids at home. It just looked like you could use a pick-me-up, and from the way you knocked it down, I'm thinking I'm right. Might just be you had a bad day, but my gut tells me that's not the case. I'm not a mind reader—I'm not even sure you're listening—but if this were just a bad day, you'd be home telling someone about it, not here, by yourself, sharing a slug with a chump like me. My guess is, the first time you came to this place, you had a bad day. But that was months ago. Maybe even years. Now, that bartender there, she knows your drink, knows when to top off, and never once has she asked you for a dime, knowing you're good for it. You'll flip her a fin on your way out, if not a ten spot, just 'cause she keeps that glass full. She ain't bad to look at, either, and if somebody asked, that's what you'd tell them, that you come here to see her. She favors the halter top, you'd say, explain that she has more tattoos than meet the eye, how once, on a slow night, she asked you to guess how many and where. I know what you're thinking: You'd rather pay me for that drink than hear another word come from my mouth. I get that. But I get that because I get you. You see, I used to be you. No one to go home to, nothing good on TV, so you find a joint with soft chairs, the game always on, nobody like me up in your face. A little patch of heaven: If only we could still smoke in here, eh? What I'm getting at is, there's no reason to be so glum. Things are going to get better. Yeah, the mayor'll fuck us with another tax hike before he's done, and if the kids keep shooting each other like this, they're going to call in the National Guard. The Cubs? Don't get me started. I just broke three pinkies at a church picnic last Sunday, dropped my cell in the toilet, and one of my kids? She's eleven and still wets the bed. But none of it's the end of the world. Somebody out there, they like you. It might be your mom. It might be your ex. It might even be our bartender, hoping and praying one day you'll buy her a drink, at another bar, in a different part of town. Heck, I like you and I don't even know you. I won't waste any more of your time, but I just wanted to say hey, introduce myself, and let you know: If you ever want to have a drink, maybe grab a bite, or just meet somewhere and talk, you're not alone. I always say: If you don't like what people are saying about you, change the conversation. And with that, I bid you adieu. *Na zdrowie.*

David Hasselhoff Enlists as an Organ Donor

Nobody lives forever. Not Brando. Not Elvis. Not Jesus. Not even the Hoff. There comes a time when a man has to look beyond his days on this Earth and consider its other inhabitants as much as he considers himself. Maybe, many a year down the road, some little blind girl in Malibu will see again thanks to these steel blue beauties. Maybe a poor refugee in El Salvador will fight for his revolution again because one of my big lungs is pumping air up into his mouth and nose. It could be a diabetic in Switzerland, producing insulin with my pancreas. A math genius at MIT discovering a new formula with my brain. Or an alcoholic mother of ten living to see her grandchildren because she has my liver pulsating inside her. My organs will pulsate inside a lot of people, I predict, save something horrific happening to my body, me burning to ash in a fire, sharks devouring me whole while I'm on vacation, kidnappers taking the ransom money and then murdering me anyway, never disclosing the location of my shallow grave. Unlikely, but anything is possible. Being me is no jog on the beach. Living life in the fast lane presents its pitfalls, its risks, a multitude of hazards. I've led a good life, been charmed many times over. Since I believe in karma, I must also believe that one of these horrible fates is due to me, that inevitably, my time is coming and coming soon. For the benefit of that little blind girl or that drunk grandma, I hope that my demise leaves the body intact, gives the surgeons—if they've got talent—something to work with, that my body can be donated to science after they've harvested every bit of me they can use for those in need. That's why I check the fire alarms for batteries once every other month. Why I don't get into strange cabs or walk alone in dark alleys. It's why I surf in large numbers, why I'll never bungee jump, skydive, or fly private jets again. When I drive, I wear my seat belt, stay at one under the speed limit, avoid the freeways like the plague. As I'm gliding along on cruise control, I can gratify myself that I'm doing my best to save the world, just keeping me intact, jeopardy waiting around every bend, the wind blowing through my hair, a voice inside my head telling me, "Good job, David. You're doing your part."

On His Deathbed, Ray Kroc Reveals the Secret Behind the Special Sauce

The CIA first contacted me in the spring of '66. At the time, a lot of their interests were tied up in South America, not to mention Vietnam, but they still had some domestic pursuits, smaller projects they'd hope to see played out, utilizing the minimum number of resources. One-man operations, hit-and-runs, that sort of thing. These plans, I would later discover, sometimes involved what many Americans would consider unnatural. Exploring ancient religions. Contacting the dead. Breeding apes with birds. The benefits of cannibalism as alternative warfare. But the biggest pot they had their hands in was mind control, bending the will of otherwise free men to serve them, do things they would never normally do, not in billions and billions of years. Subliminal messaging. Consumer tracking. Later on, microwaves from a satellite pumped directly into the brain. My contact, an Agent Lombardo, he came from the chemistry wing, and he was real interested in what people ate, and more importantly, what they ate all the time. So it was only a matter of time before this Lombardo clown knocked on my door. He wanted to know what my secret was, how I became so successful, how long I'd been working for the Russkies. Agent Lombardo laughed after he asked that last one, but I could tell he was only half-kidding. He really wanted to know if I was true to my country, and when I convinced him that I was, he wanted to know what I'd do for it. By the end of the night, we had a deal in place that would benefit both sides, give the spooks the data they wanted, give me the numbers that would make me legend. By '68, we had our agent in place. Lombardo was the chemistry whiz, and maybe the devil himself. But I know this: It was the first time in history a dab of orangish-pink would turn into so much green.

In His Last Will and Testament, John Hughes Leaves Specific Instructions for a *Breakfast Club* Sequel

The obvious choice is to set the movie at the kids' high school reunion. Why else would these five people get together again so many years later? There would be believability issues with at least two of the characters returning, but if we assume that Bender marries Claire—and we do assume this—she would talk him into going, pretty much insist. There could be an early scene where he argues about wearing a tie, about taking off his shades, about wanting to go to a reunion when nobody else liked him. Andrew would go—jocks always do—and Brian would show up, a huge success financially, a trophy wife on his arm (I'd call Diane Lane, or, if you could swing it, throw money at Nicole Kidman). Allison would be the real wildcard, because really, what does she grow up to be? What I suggest with her, and everyone, is to go the irony route. Ally is a chatty radio advice host. Claire is overweight and on welfare. Andrew gets picked on at work, à la the hairy guy he'd tormented in the locker room. Five new cliques to use as the tagline: the sad housewife, the failure, the divorcee, the midlife crisis, the heart attack waiting to happen. The real key, though, is to get them all in the library, and for some reason, make it so they can't leave. It wouldn't be a stretch for this high school to have alarmed doors, not since Columbine, so maybe they could take a walk, or maybe they could all make a series of wrong turns. Then when they try to leave, the door is armed and they're stuck. That's when it would all come out, how their seemingly perfect lives are not so perfect, how the faces they put on aren't who they really are. There would be dramatic monologues. There would be tears. Tempers would rise, spurring at least two fights. Somebody would kiss someone—Brian and Allison jump out at me—and it's logical to have at least one of them divorced and another with cancer, whatever cancer needs the publicity, something we could give 1 percent of the box to. And of course there'd be music, a mix of the original songs and what the kids like today, something new in the opening credits, Simple Minds at the climax, a remix pumping through the speakers as our five heroes gallop through the hallways, evading responsibility, working together as a team, just trying to find their way back home.

The Water Tower Suffers Post-Traumatic Stress Disorder

Imagine everyone you've ever known, all your family and friends, dying in one fell swoop. Imagine their deaths coming quickly, one after another like dominos, but being horrible and excruciating, burning them alive in a wave of hysteria. Imagine believing the same death was coming for you, surrounding you, denying any mercy, promising to take you last. First, you'd have to witness its power, watch what it did to all your friends, all the while standing there helpless, impotent, no way to keep yourself from watching their agony. Their cries are audible only to you, so many people about, bells clanging, panic as thick as fog, the city being laid to waste. Imagine feeling the flames on your back, on your face, seeing them approach, knowing what had happened to everyone else was about to befall you. Surely you are thinking of the relief of being saved, the water finally winning out, your place in history secure: the lone survivor. I'll even bet you think I'm lucky. But then imagine the guilt. Imagine being the last one, carrying the burden of being spared. On top of that, imagine all the appearances, the photo ops, the interviews, all those questions, everyone asking for you to relive the moment, to describe what it was like, to provide a detailed account of your friends' demise. When the dust settled, imagine what it would have been like to see everyone replaced, to watch their proxies rise, for everyone to whisper how these new friends were better, thinking you couldn't hear, maybe not caring. Imagine becoming the symbol of something lost, a dead era, once a beacon of progress, now just a link to the past. Maybe you think I should have moved on by now. Maybe I should accept my role. Maybe you think I'm pathetic. And maybe you think because I'm made of stone I can't still feel the heat, hear the fire roar. But if you imagine only one thing, imagine this: Just because I'm full of water doesn't mean I can't burn.

In Hell, H.H. Holmes and John Wayne Gacy Talk Shit About Richard Speck's Tits

At first we thought they were part of his punishment. It's the kind of thing they do down here, to make things worse, because it amuses them. We've seen guys with dicks for noses and cheese for eyes and badgers for asses and asses for feet. Even *we* think some of the shit they come up with is pretty messed up. But after knowing Richard five, ten years—time doesn't mean much down here—he casually dropped it into a conversation: "I had these when I arrived. I got them in prison." Immediately, when he saw the grins on our faces, he knew he'd made a fatal error. To be clear, there's nothing much that happens around here to make our situation any better. This is Hell, and on a continuous basis, we are in agony, both mental and physical, the people in charge creating new ways to make our existence redefine the term "suffering." But every once in a while, when we least expect it, an inconsistency in the routine—that's what we'll call it—comes along and relieves the pain, soothes the burden, just a little bit, just for an instant. Richard's self-induced breasts did just that. Don't get us wrong: In our situation, we've learned a lot about acceptance, a lot about differing perspectives, and if we'd had time to stop and think, we might not have snickered the way we did. We know that some people can't help what they look like, and more so, we understand certain people opt to look a certain way and we shouldn't resort to traditional standards of beauty. Personal appearance is no reason to pass judgment. It's not like either of us would look the way we do if we had a chance to do it all again. But really, Richard should have known better. He's in Hell and he was talking to us. At first, we didn't believe him. We thought he was kidding or just pulling our legs; we'd heard people deny punishments before, play the by-choice card, trying to save face in front of the guys. But the look on his pock-marked face told us he was serious—he was claiming this shit, owning up like someone says they're a blond or a teenage boy. We jabbed at him, told him he was full of it, but he stuck to his story, said he had them done for a guy, said he was doing a lot of drugs, kept going back and forth. We pressed on: "Was it for a guy or because you were doing a lot of drugs?" Richard also added weird, inconsistent details, changing how he got them, what the guy's name was, adding things like "I swear!" to the end of every sentence. Our disbelief took on another meaning: We were sure he had them when he got here, but we weren't so sure they were his idea. For one, why tits? For two, why tits? On top of all that, we started to point out that they weren't particularly attractive tits, and then things really took off. We started using some nasty, hurtful nicknames: “Sweet Potatoes” or “Saggamuffin” or “Jacques Marquette” (inside joke). It got to be so bad, he didn’t want to be around us anymore, even going so far as to ask to be moved, which was his second mistake, as, well, he was missing the point. In the end, a person has a lot of regrets, and Richard telling us what he told us would have to rank up right up there on his list. Sooner or later, we’ll either let up or he’ll get used to it, but in the meantime, we’re still going to leave old bras in his locker, we’re still going to point to the ground and ask him what they’re looking at, and we’re still going to give him hard, relentless titty-twisters, even when he begs us to stop, even when it’s not funny anymore.

Nathan Leopold Explains the Ferris Wheel to Richard Loeb, Wolf Lake, 1924

The most common misconception about the Ferris Wheel is that it is named after the Latin for iron, "ferrous," instead of its true eponym, modern creator and constructor George Washington Gale Ferris, Jr., though the homonymic qualities certainly render the mistake understandable. Another fact most people don't know is the concept had been around for centuries before the Columbian Exposition. After all, what is a water wheel but a Ferris wheel, a Ferris wheel to rotate water instead of persons? Primitive drawings of a passenger-carrying wheels litter history, crude rope-and-axle sketches from darker times, darker places, Turkey most prominently. In their age, they were called "pleasure wheels," turned by simple men for the enjoyment of the wealthy and dignified. Can you imagine these savages facing famine and war and genocide, yet they'd be subjugated to spinning their princes and dukes about, purely for the thrill of the ride? An outstanding concept, certainly, but what of the modern equivalent? Mr. Coolidge twirling about like a kite in the breeze while shirtless underlings sweat in the grime below, for instance. Why should the most respected and powerful man in our great nation not symbolically place himself above those who are lesser than he? In an ideal society, presidents, kings, and scholars would employ the wonders of science at their whim, those beneath them acquiescing to their wills. The Ferris Wheel, in that light, serves not only as a symbol of our great city, but of our nation, of progress, of better times, of a more civilized society. Most of its citizens will not recognize the parallel, let alone surrender themselves to its genius, but their role is not to understand, only obey. Our nation's journey toward greatness will be one filled with challenges, many forks in its proverbial road. What those of us meant for greatness must never forget, never lose sight of, is that wherever you start, no matter where you've traveled, that's where you'll ultimately return.

Pat Sajak Explains the Many Metaphors of a Giant Spinning Wheel

Firstly, the Earth itself spins on an axis. In fact, everything in the universe spins, unless you're at the very center of the sun. In that way, the wheel itself is a microcosm of us all. And that's just one aspect. Making the wheel so small, and with handles, illustrates man's attempt to manipulate the world, while the randomness of his success proves our existential nature, how we really have so little control. Further, doesn't everything, no matter how far away it goes or how fast it travels, always come back to us? It could be trouble. It could be a bad penny. If we're lucky? Love. Moving right along, if you'll recall, man's first invention—before fire, by some accounts—is the wheel, what we associate as the birth of engineering, man's conquest over nature, our attempt to control the universe. Speaking of which, "Spinning your wheels" is also one of our more popular adages, one that evokes the image of gears moving throughout the head (in place of the brain), thought itself the by-product of a semi-complex machine, moving parts rolling about each other, perpetuating motion, i.e., ideas. Time, which we are all slaves to, is controlled by clocks, run by the same inner workings of gears. Sometimes I take things further and project myself into the clockmaker's role, one theory of the creator of the universe. In this version,

God merely sets the game into motion and watches as the players fulfill their own destiny, using the tools they've been given, following a distinct set of rules. Sure, once in a while, I step in to move things along, but for the most part, the wheel dictates all. The wheel decides who lives and who dies, gives us choices, indiscriminately takes them away. The wheel simultaneously guides us along, encourages us, and destroys us, but never gives us the answers, hoping that we keep asking, keep searching, confident that one day, on our own, we'll fill in the blanks.

In a Prerecorded Message Played at His Hall of Fame Induction, Ron Santo Outlines the Inevitable Cubs World Series Championship Parade

Instead of ending in Grant Park, this parade will start in Grant Park. That will give us a large, centralized place for everyone to meet. There's going to be a lot of people in this parade. The players would be first, everyone on a big blue float, sequins shining in the October sun, everyone waving, drinking champagne, and blowing kisses to the crowd, all of them trying and failing to hold back the tears. After that, they'd have to have former Cubs, and by that, I mean all of them. Ernie gets his own car, a blue Chevy convertible, Billy and Fergie, too. Then Ryno, Hawk, Mad Dog, and maybe a couple of other guys, Beckert and Kessinger and my pal, Hundley. Gracie and Sutcliffe and heck, Sammy Sosa, too. After that, there could be more floats, enough for anyone who's ever played for the Cubs, whether they had one at-bat or they served faithfully for years, never getting a statue, never getting their number on the foul pole. Next would be the owners, along with all the executives, broadcasters, scouts, office staff, anyone else who had anything to do with the team's success, the people who put it all together. Security guys, groundskeepers, scorekeepers, ushers, janitors, vendors, the guys in the clubhouse, they'd be next, all in uniform, all waving to the fans, maybe throwing little pieces of candy to the kids, holding up their fingers, mouthing *We're number 1!* After that, anyone who wanted to join in, anyone who's suffered, anyone who endured, anyone who made it through to the end, they could all follow, even those who lost hope, even those who never followed the team, everyone everywhere, one big, citywide parade. From Grant Park we'll move up Michigan Avenue, cross the river, wave hello to everyone at the Wrigley Building and Tribune Tower, point at whoever is in the WGN booth, give them a thumbs-up as they call play-by-play. We'd go up Lake Shore—they'd have to close the whole city down—all the way to North Avenue and cut through Lincoln Park. Everyone would give a speech, and then we'd head up Clark toward the Field, stopping at the Billy Goat along the way to say hello, to tell everyone there are no hard feelings. Once we make it to Wrigley, we'll do three laps around, one for every championship so far, the stadium full to the gills with anyone who wanted to come in and feel the energy, exorcise their ghosts, see the flag flying high on the center field pole. Then we'll work our way back south, all the way past Downtown, all the way to Comiskey and do a lap there, just to say hello to the fans on the South Side, let them know that we did it, that we love them just as much as we can love anyone. Finally, we'll end up back at Grant Park, and there, the parade will end and the party will begin. Everyone will get up on stage, and everyone, no matter who they are, will get a chance to talk. The whole shebang might take three days, a modern Woodstock, fans drunk on Old Style, sleeping in tents, lots of free love, no one wanting to go home, not until it's over, not until the final peanut vendor says *thank you,* not until Monday comes and the mayor make us leave. We could stay forever, we know, just celebrate until we die, but eventually, we'd have to get back to it. After all, what would be sweeter than the next Cubs' World Series title? Two World Series titles! Our second repeat, and after that, what Cub fans deserve, what's been long overdue, a Cub dynasty to last the ages, nothing but total and complete domination.

Steve Dahl Dreams of Demolitions That Never Were

Disco was only the beginning. Without a doubt, it could have been an annual event. We could have blown crap up once a week, at least at every Friday home game, extra performances on holidays. Music didn't stop sucking when the leisure suits and platforms went out of style: Music has sucked consistently since then. In fact, music has broken off into sub-genres of suck, enough suck to go around so that everyone gets a little suck of their own. When disco died, they came up with New Wave and every limey weirdo with a keyboard and a keytar and a piano key skinny tie got a record contract, so many records I would have loved to blow up. Boy bands weren't too far behind, not that these little urchins were bands at all, just a bunch of latchkey babies who weren't good at sports and too much gel in their hair and no pubes on their nuts. Supposedly, grunge came along and "saved" music, but I have a special powder keg in my heart for those flannel-wearing mopes singing with marbles in their mouths. And don't get me started on rap: If I hadn't been banned from Comiskey, I certainly would have been run out of town, all those white kids driving around Naperville in their dads' LeBaron convertibles, blasting that bass, bobbing their heads like they're headed for a drive-by at the Old Navy. Country? We're a thousand miles north of where it should be legal to play country music. Ska? Please. Folk? No thanks. Jazz? Try writing some lyrics. No matter what the fad, the flavor of the month, I would have been ready, a stick of dynamite in one hand and a gift card to Borders in the other. People called me racist for what I did to disco, people called me homophobic, people say I incited a riot. Some people got hurt. I say that's collateral damage. If I could do it again, just one more time, I'd light a fire they could see from New York, from Los Angeles, from the studios where they concoct all this shitty "music." I'd blow up cassettes. I'd blow up CDs. I'd blow up iPods and iPads and cell phones, knocking out all those crappy ringtones in the process. I'd charge ten cents for beer and yell for everyone to storm the field. I'd raffle off the chance to light the fuse. I'd make peace with Garry and then blow him up, too. I'd make the airwaves safe for decent people. I'd save them from their own suckiness. I'd change the world. Again.

Upon Rhubarb's Death, Ribbie Laments Never Being Honest About His True Feelings

The readiest I ever felt was the day they asked us to clean out our lockers. It'd already been a couple years at that point, and I'd backed down a thousand times before. But that day, that was the day. The waiting was worse than anything that could happen, I'd convinced myself, and acknowledged we weren't getting any younger. I dreamed of how our lives might change, the media's response, how the brass would react to the news—would they insist upon secrecy? Then, when the decision came down, us on the other side of the ledger, my timing seemed even more perfect. Change was in the air. Transition. On our way out of the office, in the cool, dark tunnels underneath the park, I prepared myself for purging, for whatever was to follow. But it was you who made a move (it always was), stopping us mid-stride, grabbing my wrist, staring up into my eyes. I thought, for that brief moment before you spoke, you were thinking what I was, that for years, we'd been afraid of each other. We'd laugh at the time we'd wasted, move forward and never look back. But the words that came from your mouth echoed no sentiment I'd ever experienced: "Let's call Jimmy Pearsall." Three days later, still vomiting and smelling of Southern Comfort, I called your number, but you'd already disconnected the line. I could have found you, asked at the stadium where they were forwarding your last check, but I didn't. If you'd wanted that, dreamed what I dreamed, felt what I felt, you wouldn't have left without saying good-bye.

SOX

Sister Carrie Facebooks Frankie Machine

What made me click his profile was his eyes. There's sadness there, behind a facade of confidence, but sadness nonetheless. There's also something in his posture, the kind of weariness a man isn't born with, but can only accumulate. All of it called out, *Now Caroline, there's a man worth a gander.* Maybe it's the camera, maybe it's the angle, or maybe someone just caught him at a bad moment. But remember, he chose that picture to represent himself. We're talking free will, after all: He wants the world to see what I'm seeing, wants everyone to know his pain, to reach out, to help him grow stronger. Of course, he has a wife, and that's swell, but he doesn't seem so high on her, either, with what he posts, and more so, what he doesn't. In nearly twelve hundred photos—most in a bar, I might add—only a handful depict the lovely Mrs. Majcinek, and nary a one features them together. It is not my intention to impede upon their love, though that territory is not unfamiliar to me. It is just the nature of the beast, this Facebook, to bring such opportunities to light, to forge friendships of this nature. Reaching out to this man, to those eyes, may lead to him accepting friendship, and from there, who knows? A poke here, a like there, and before you know it, you find out if that friend is worthy of further pokes and further likes.

Before long, the right needling can lead to messages, to suggestions, and if the winds blow right, actual human contact. I, too, am betrothed, but for now, all of this is innocent, a friendly hand reaching out. Eventually, though, this could be the man to swoop me off my feet, carry me forward, initiate nothing short of a positive change in my status.

Roger Ebert Critiques His Second Date With Oprah Winfrey

At the movie, I realized how terrible an idea it was to go to a movie. Considering how well the first date went, sitting, talking, eating, why wouldn't I go back to the same plan, what each of us did so well? If it ain't broke, right? You can't talk at a movie—I'd sooner die than break that rule—so I chose the one place we couldn't converse, where I couldn't let my best attributes come to light. I also ran the risk of coming off as a know-it-all. People go to the movies to laugh, to cry, to be scared, to be entertained. But intimidated? I should have thought it out. Despite everything, things started well enough. I took her to a sneak preview, which I thought would impress her, and truthfully, I think it did. She'd never been to a critics' screening, she said, and I thought that perhaps I'd made a good decision after all. We got some popcorn and some sodas, sat in the back row, near the door, where I could use the light to take notes. When the lights went down is when things went south. While a movie might not have been such a bad idea, the particular movie is what ultimately did me in. A romance would have been ideal, while an action movie would have been fun. Even a scary movie could have been good, her moving closer, squeezing my hand, hiding her face in my arm. But no, it was a comedy, and not just any comedy, but a sex comedy. The movie that was screening that night? *Revenge of the Nerds*. At first, it wasn't so bad. "Nerd," it seemed, was synonymous with "successful," not to mention "bespectacled," and while I was the only one with glasses, we had both studied hard, attained a level of success that would have branded us both, by anyone's standards, nerds. But then I dug myself deeper, early on, when I whispered into her ear (breaking my sacred rule), "These guys remind me of me." I was just trying to have fun, somewhat at my own expense. But when it became obvious that these boys were nothing like me, that they were crude and uncouth—and that there'd be lots and lots of nudity—I cringed. By the time the panty raid scene ended and the nerds were watching the sorority girls undress on live video feeds, we couldn't have been farther apart if there was a seat between us. I saw her looking down at her watch. I saw her averting her eyes. I saw the look of disgust. I pretended to take notes, start my column. But really, there wasn't much to say. It was what it was: Underdogs want to get laid, underdogs get laid, pure escapist fantasy. I could have written the review without seeing the movie. After, when the cab pulled up to her building, I asked if she wanted to grab a bite, maybe a drink. She cited what time she had to be in the makeup chair. I vaulted out and scurried around the back of the taxi, trying to open her door for her, wondering if there'd be any chance of a goodnight peck. On my way, I tripped over my own feet, fell to the street. I looked up to see her walk away, heard her faint "Thank you" and "Good night." I could see her feet under the car parked next to the curb. She was making tracks. Then, not knowing where I was, what I was doing, the cabbie pulled away, left me there. I looked ridiculous. There was no speech to save me, not like in the movie. No sweet redemption, no happy ending. I stood up and started walking home, my building not that far. I remember feeling so clumsy, so awkward. Oafish and ham-handed, gawkish and graceless. Just another nerd, all bungle, all blunder. All thumbs.

In His New Infomercial for Male Enhancement Tablets, Mr. T Feels Pity for the Foolish Consumer Who Does Not Call Now

If you could get it up, you wouldn't be watching me right now. Only a sucker is up this late, the TV on, no lady to grab onto and turn the lights out with. That's why I'm talking to you now. Take this pill and you won't be a momma's boy anymore. Get yourself a ladyfriend. Get some lovin'. Get some sleep. All you got to do is call the number on the screen, talk to one of my friends standing by. They'll hook you up. In four to six weeks, you'll be up late, but not watching me. You'll be solid gold. You'll be A-Team. The ladies won't keep their hands off you. Not when you take this pill. It sends a message to your brain, sends it loud and clear: *Heart, send some blood down south. Do it now.* Bam, you're a man again. Take it from me, Mr. T. Even he has rocky times. But no more. I took the pill. My friends are standing by. All major credit cards accepted. Call now. Get up and call now. Take it from T.

Minna and Ada Everleigh Reveal What Possibly Could Have Happened to Marshall Field, Jr.

We were downstairs. Our job was to oversee the operation, meet and greet the clients, make sure everyone was having a good time, and most of all, keep the money coming in. We were entrepreneurs, after all, good at what we did. We also trusted that our girls knew what they were doing when they entertained; otherwise, they wouldn't have been our girls: pretty in the face, smart in the head. All we can honestly relay is what we heard, what we were told, and what the papers reported afterward. So, firstly, what we heard was a loud noise. Someone, a policeman, for instance, might mistake this noise for a gunshot. Others, though, might call it a champagne cork popping from a bottle, one of several dozen popped every night. Others could say a headboard banged against a wall, which nobody would debate. We also know the man in question was on the premises—he frequented our services, proved a valuable business contact, many of the fine amenities on hand coming from the store bearing his name—but we cannot say for sure he was present on the night in question, let alone upstairs, in the Gold Room or the gambling parlor. We know that the victim died soon after the alleged incident, but five days after, in his own home instead of a hospital, and to us, that doesn't indicate a fatal wound could have incurred whilst in our care.

We also know the victim was prone to depression—pillow talk, don't you know—and would have had access to a number of firearms, the means, the motive, and the opportunity. We also know that no one under our employ was charged, let alone arrested, and the alleged questioning that took place? Well, a lot of men talk to our girls, about a lot of things; questions may indeed have been asked and answered. No blood-stained sheets or mattresses were ever found or confiscated, and if an extensive search took place, no bullet holes were discovered. What we think happened to Mr. Field in our house is that he enjoyed our services, contributed to the local economy, and left with a smile on his face. We've seen that. We can attest to it. We know it to be true. And we're sticking with our story.

Jane Addams Leaves Hull House for 5 Bedrooms and 3.5 Baths in Lush Suburban New Lenox

If there's one thing I'm tired of, it's other people's problems. This one's husband didn't come home last night. This one's husband drinks too much. This one's husband _________. Enough already. When is someone going to ask *me* what's wrong? Inquire about *my* feelings? I've made my own bed, I know, but there's only so much you can take before it gets to you, before you just have to get out. On the other hand, here are some things I'll never get tired of: cathedral ceilings. Cherry hardwood floors. French double doors. Bay windows. My own bathroom, a step-in spa off in the corner. Walk-in closets the size of three bus stops. Sleeping in a quiet room, on a bed, all by myself. It wasn't too hard to convince myself I'd earned this, ten times over. At least. And besides, how long could it be before one of the forty-something trophy wives from up the block knocks on my door, asks me over for coffee, and like I had a sign on my forehead, tells me she's alone in the world, explains why she always wears sunglasses, even at night. Even indoors.

Eating William Wells' Stout Heart, Fort Dearborn, 1812

In your hand, it feels like it's still beating. The hardest part isn't the kill, or the careful removal with a dull knife. It's shaking the notion that you're about to consume something alive, something whole, that it might scream out in horror when you break the skin with your teeth. Picture holding a small animal between your thumbs and pointers—a squirrel, a bat, a pike—then biting down into its shoulder. It is warm, full of blood, and trying its best to slip free, to claw you to shreds. The only thing that makes you go through with it is your audience, everyone waiting for their turn, wanting their share of bravery, strength, and verisimilitude. Deep down, you know they're thinking the same thing you are, that there are better paths to self-improvement. But first in line is an honor; you get the best piece, the most potent hunk. Your tribesmen aren't the only ones watching, either. There are the others, behind the wall, witnessing why they call you savage firsthand. It becomes a pissing match at that point—who can be more turned off by what you've done, by what you're about to do. You start to wonder if this is the only way to work out your differences, and then, as your hand drips red, you swear you feel another pulse. In the end, you know you'll go through with it. That you have no choice. Otherwise, it would be an awful waste.

Unearthed at an Archaeological Dig, the Shawon-O-Meter Speaks to the Media, Harry Caray's Tavern, 2169

It's true what they say, how you don't realize how much you miss everyone until you're gone. The sad thing is when you look around and everyone you knew and loved is dead, not to mention forgotten. The last time I saw Shawon, let alone anyone else from the old days, he was getting up there, so I had a feeling, even before they told me just how long I was away, that his time had passed. Still, there's nothing you can do to prepare yourself, not even with a century in a scrap heap to mull it over. I'll be in mourning for a while, surely, but there's also a lot to be excited about. Firstly, over a century's worth of seasons to catch up on, rooms full of tape to watch, lots of box scores to rifle through. I've been grateful for your cooperation, not letting on, not giving anything away. When I do sit down, I'm going to start at the beginning, trace the steps in order, see if I can't experience things the way I would have had I never left. I don't want the highlights; I want it all, the ups, the downs, the tragedies, the triumphs. I'm hoping for the best, of course, for happy endings to more than one story. Best-case scenario: We've caught the Yanks, fly as many banners, if not more, than those goons from the Bronx. Maybe we've lapped them. Maybe more. Worst-case scenario: I find just one flag, one shining moment, one title that ended the grief, the misery, the streak. Now many of you are probably saying to yourself, *That's not the worst case scenario, Shawon-O-Meter,* trying to avoid eye contact, feeling a pain for me in your hearts. But if that's the case, then what you're thinking is unthinkable. Why would you unearth me if that was the news you had to give? Why not just burn me up and scatter my ashes under the St. Louis Arch? No, just one championship, over so many years, is the worst-case scenario. But I'll find that out ... in due time. First, I'm going to visit some old friends, drop by a few graves, lift a few cold ones in their honor. Then I'm going to start with some videos of the games I was at, see myself in the crowd, younger, less peaked, vacillating with every AB. I can't wait to see the sun, to hear Harry do the lineup, to feel the roar of the crowd at the slightest hint of something positive. More than anything, I'm going to be on the lookout for number 12, a ground ball to the left side, my man snatching it, winding up, launching a 100-mph fastball toward Gracey, missing completely, and seeing those fans along the first base line scatter, duck and cover, run as if for their very lives.

SHAWON-O-METER

.278

ANDRKSING.GOCUBS

Intrigued by Reincarnation, Skip Dillard Embraces Buddhism

When you have a next life, there's no such thing as a one-on-one. The concept of not getting a second chance after failing on the first is so Western, it's no wonder we're always at war. Imagine a world where redemption is only a step off the roof away. Tripping in front of a bus would do it, too, and so would two bottles of Tylenol. A hungry bear in the woods. A lucky bolt of lightning. Colon cancer. No matter what you were guilty of, or innocent, you could start over any time you wanted. Sure, a margin of error exists. You could come back as an infectious microbe. A sickly leopard. The maggot born in the trash can behind some Chinese take-out joint. But you might get lucky, too, end up rich, a beautiful actress, married to a handsome athlete, always on the news for her charitable tendencies. You could be a famous doctor. An inventor. The first man to do something no one's ever done before, like walk on Mars or travel back in time. You could be the lap dog to that same beautiful actress, traveling in her purse, your picture in a thousand magazines, a kiss on the nose for every flash of the camera. Even better, you could be nobody. You could go about your business, live your life. Minor victories would go unnoticed, as would major defeats. Even if anyone turned around to look, it wouldn't matter. Either you wouldn't care, or you'd move on again, the next roll of the dice. If you kept shooting, sooner or later, you'd get better at it, always get something good. Like you were money in the bank.

In a Séance at Playboy's 100th Anniversary Party, Hugh Hefner Speaks on Sex in the Afterlife

Are you seriously asking? I could tell you, but think about it: Do you really want to know? I mean, mysteries are called mysteries for a reason: You're not supposed to know, and trust me, I don't think you want to know. Besides, have you considered the possibility that maybe I'm not the best basis of comparison? Considering my experiences on Earth, I have a slightly skewed idea of normal. My standards were, after all, abnormally high. I had a pretty good run, one might say, so afterward, what could I expect? To be honest, I went in with no expectations. I couldn't complain, could I? And I certainly couldn't expect an upgrade. At best, I hoped to continue. Remember, if I went by Judeo-Christian standards, nothing short of doom awaited my arrival at the party. Thankfully, I wasn't going by Judeo-Christian standards. So you could say I was optimistic, ready for anything. But if you really want to know, and it seems like you really do, I'll tell you this, and let you figure it out for yourself: Think back to the first time you ever made love, or more poignantly, were about to make love, that feeling of anticipation welling, a tear that just won't make it over the hump of your cheek. Think of the moment when you knew that your partner (or partners) was ready, was willing, that all your preconceptions, everything you'd heard—from parents, teachers, your big brother, TV and movies, adult magazines, anyone you knew—nothing even remotely prepared you for that moment; nothing they said, nothing you saw, nothing you heard could scratch the surface of what you were thinking. How it couldn't even approach the instant when you made contact with your partner, confident in what was about to happen, knowing that you were no longer going to be a virgin, that you were entering the realm of the sexually active, that you were a member of that club that once seemed impossible to join, the club that, as Groucho once said, you wouldn't want to be in because they'd have you as a member. Now try to recapture that feeling of fear turning into joy turning into elation turning into wild abandon, into passion, into mindless, animal sex. You and your partner becoming one, your membership in the club approved for platinum status. That fear, that happiness, that elation, that feeling of belonging to someone who would have you, the greatest moment in your and everyone else's life. Do you remember that? Well, it's nothing like sex in the afterlife.

WITH NOTHING LEFT TO PROVE, OPRAH WINFREY JOINS THE CAST OF SECOND CITY

As the saying goes, nothing's harder than comedy. Interviews. Movie producing. Acting. Publishing. Even drastic weight loss. It's all a bowl of cake compared to making people laugh. But, like any of the above, I'm not only going to hold my own, I'm going to knock them dead. For example, in an upcoming sketch, I play a fire hydrant. While my previous roles have for the most part thrust me into the mindset of a former slave looking to overcome, this role calls for greater range. I'm red, I'm still, and I'm preyed upon by a nervous Irish setter. Now, the casual observer might see a connection between Sparky the Sparkplug and my Sethe, the oppression, the inability to act, the humiliation, etc., and even Stedman calls it creative typecasting. But I call it opportunity. Stanislavsky tells the actor to become the role, lose the self, be your character. Only then can you act. On center stage, the spotlight beating down on me, the crowd's expectations higher than normal, all I can do is be that fire hydrant. I will possess its redness. Embrace the stillness. Accept my fate, be it chipped paint, inclement weather, and the occasional canine. I will relish hot summer days, cooling children with a rhythmic spray. I will double as a bike rack. Above all, I will fulfill my destiny, perhaps one day save lives, smoke billowing like a beacon of destiny. No matter what, I'll be ready. Red and still. Awaiting fire.

From the Grave, Carl Sandburg Workshops the Author's Manuscript (sans this last page)

Word butcher for the world. Tool. Stacker of cliché. Stormy, husky, brooding, Assumer of Big Shoulders. You are wicked, and everyone will believe me. Your patterns of imagery lie crooked yet you write and go free to write again. I may be brutal but my reply is: I have seen the marks of wanton prose. I turn yet again to you, who sneers at this my city, I give you back the sneer and say: Your tongue is coarse and strong, lapping for action verbs, for controlling metaphor. Your prose, bareheaded; shoveling; wrecking; building; breaking. The inconsistency of each voice leaves me laughing, laughing with decayed teeth, laughing under the terrible burden of honesty: you suck. No pulse under his wrist, no heart under his ribs. I am just grateful that I didn't show up in any of these.

About the Author

Michael Czyzniejewski was born in Chicago and grew up in its south suburbs. He teaches at Bowling Green State University and serves as Editor-in-Chief of the *Mid-American Review*. He is also the author of the story collection *Elephants in Our Bedroom* (Dzanc Books, 2009), and in 2010, received a Literature Fellowship from the National Endowment for the Arts. Michael lives in Bowling Green with his wife and son, returning to Chicago each summer to sell beer in the aisles of Wrigley Field.

www.michaelczyzniejewski.com

Author photo by Jacob Knabb.

ACKNOWLEDGEMENTS

The author would like to thank the editors of the following publications, in which some of the preceding stories have previously appeared (in some cases, with slightly different titles).

Another Chicago Magazine

"David Yow's 10 Simple Rules for Keeping a Smile on Your Face"

"Dennis Rodman Envisions His Last Tattoo"

"During a Brief Commerical Break, Wizzo the Wizard Pitches a Rock Opera/Concept Album to Special Guest Billy Corgan"

"Eating William Wells' Stout Heart, Fort Dearborn, 1812"

"In His Best-Selling Autobiography, Dennis DeYoung Reveals the Origins of 'Come Sail Away'"

"In His New Infomercial for Male Enhancement Tablets, Mr. T Feels Pity for the Foolish Consumer Who Does Not Call Now"

"Mayor Daley Confronts Frank Gehry in the Men's Room at the Michigan Avenue Bennigan's"

"Mrs. O'Leary's Ghost Comforts Steve Bartman at the Ruins of Meigs Field"

"On His Deathbed, Ray Kroc Reveals the Secret Behind the Special Sauce"

"Roger Ebert Critiques His Second Date With Oprah Winfrey"

"With Nothing Left to Prove, Oprah Winfrey Joins the Cast of Second City"

Artifice

"Barack Obama Describes His Perfect Bowling Game to the Graduating Class, Arizona State University Commencement, 2029"

"In a Séance at Playboy's 100th Anniversary Party, Hugh Hefner Speaks on Sex in the Afterlife"

"Rod Blagojevich Negotiates His First Prison Tattoo, Joliet State Penitentiary"

The Collagist

"Gil Scott-Heron Leaves a Voice Mail for R. Kelly, February 3, 2002"

"Jean Baptiste Point du Sable Settles at the Mouth of the Cuyahoga River"

"Nathan Leopold Explains the Ferris Wheel to Richard Loeb, Wolf Lake, 1924"

Knee-Jerk

"In His Last Will and Testament, John Hughes Leaves Specific Instructions for a *Breakfast Club* Sequel"

"Intrigued by Reincarnation, Skip Dillard Embraces Buddhism"

"Jane Addams Leaves Hull House for 5 Bedrooms and 3.5 Baths in Lush Suburban New Lenox"

"Speaking at the Calumet City Chamber of Commerce Annual Luncheon, Gary Dotson Tells Tale of Inspiration and Longing"

"Tired of the Spaceship Comparisons, the New Soldier Field Responds to Its Critics"

"Upon Rhubarb's Death, Ribbie Laments Never Being Honest About His True Feelings"

Make

"John Wentworth Defends the Potential Awesomeness of Chicago, Wisconsin"

"Steve Dahl Dreams of Demolitions That Never Were"

"The Water Tower Suffers Post-Traumatic Stress Disorder"

The Nervous Breakdown

"Pat Sajak Explains the Many Metaphors of a Giant Spinning Wheel"

Ninth Letter Online

"The Ghost of Rosetta Jackson Lobbies Congress to Continue Funding Planned Parenthood"

"In a Prerecorded Message Played at His Hall of Fame Induction, Ron Santo Outlines the Inevitable Cubs World Series Championship Parade"

"The Sixteen-Inch Softball Buys a Shot of Malort for the Italian Beef Sandwich at the End of the Bar"

The Packingtown Review

"Jane Byrne Discusses Edward Hopper's *Nighthawks* With Her New Neighbors, Cabrini-Green, 1981"

Requited

"Ann Landers Advises Against the Use of Twitter"

"Minna and Ada Everleigh Reveal What Possibly Could Have Happened to Marshall Field, Jr."

"Sister Carrie Facebooks Frankie Machine"

The author would like to acknowledge the following people, all of whom have supported this project: Debt to everyone at Curbside Splendor, especially Victor David Giron, Ben Tanzer, and Leah Tallon. Additional thanks go to the editors of the magazines who accepted individual stories for their publications: James Tadd Adcox, Matt Bell, Casey Bye-Jon Fullmer-Steve Tartaglione, Kamilah Foreman, Tasha Fouts, Gina Frangello, Amanda Marbais, and Jodee Stanley. Gratitude to the blurbists: Allison Amend, Gina Frangello, Lindsay Hunter, Alan Heathcock, Billy Lombardo, John McNally, and Bayo Ojikutu, great Chicago writers, all. Admiration to Rob Funderburk for bringing vision to my thoughts. Love goes to Karen and Ernie for enabling and inspiring me to write. Heartfelt appreciation goes to Jacob Knabb, who was on this from the beginning, who saw it through. This book would not exist without the help of everyone involved.

Also available from Curbside Splendor

Piano Rats by Franki Elliot

The Chapbook: Poems by Charles Bane, Jr.

Sophomoric Philosophy by Victor David Giron

The Curbside Splendor semi-annual collection of short stories and poetry

www.curbsidesplendor.com

CPSIA information can be obtained at www.ICGtesting.com
Printed in the USA
LVOW110500170512

282126LV00005B/3/P